Katie and the Puppy Next Door

John Himmelman

Henry Holt and Company ♥ New York

Henry Holt and Company, LLC
PUBLISHERS SINCE 1866
175 Fifth Avenue
New York, New York 10010
mackids.com

Library of Congress Cataloging-in-Publication Data
Himmelman, John.
Katie and the puppy next door / John Himmelman. — 1st ed.
    p.   cm.
Summary: Katie the dog learns that sharing can be fun when she
becomes friends with the playful puppy next door.
ISBN 978-0-8050-9484-8 (hardcover)
[1. Dogs—Fiction. 2. Animals—Infancy—Fiction.
3. Sharing—Fiction. 4. Friendship—Fiction.] I. Title.
PZ7.H5686Kap 2013   [E]—dc23   2012006323

First Edition—2013
The artist used black Prismacolor pencils and watercolors
to create the illustrations for this book.
Printed in China by South China Printing Company Ltd.,
Dongguan City, Guangdong Province

1 3 5 7 9 10 8 6 4 2

For Sally and sweet little Jezelle
—J. H.

One morning, at breakfast time, Sara Ann said,
"Guess what, Katie? Our new neighbors,
Elizabeth and Ruby, are coming over!"

Katie did not know who they were, but she
wagged her tail politely.

When the doorbell rang, Sara Ann called Katie to the door. "Come meet your new friend," she said.

"Yip! Yip! Yip!" barked Ruby. She
ran past Katie and into the house.

Katie found her playing with the cats.

The cats are MY friends, not hers!
Katie thought. She burst into the room.
"Woof! Woof!" she barked.

Ruby ran into the kitchen.
She started to eat Katie's food.

That is MY food! thought Katie.
"Woof! Woof!" she barked.
   Ruby took another bite and ran out
of the kitchen.

Katie looked for Ruby. She found her
chewing on HER squeaky bone!

"Woof! Woof!" she barked. Ruby dropped the bone and hid under the couch.

Katie took her toy and began to chew. She didn't feel like playing with it, but she didn't want Ruby to have it, either.

Sara Ann came into the room. "Oh, Katie," she said. "You should share your things with your friends. That's what makes having friends fun."

Elizabeth picked up Ruby and took her home.

The next week, Sara Ann said, "Katie, Elizabeth and Ruby are coming over again today. Please try to share your things."

Katie left the room and lay down on her pillow. She did not want to share her things. They were HER things!

Later, Katie heard noises in the other
room. Ruby was playing with the cats. "Woof!"
barked Katie. She was about to burst into the
room and chase Ruby away. She tried to hold
herself back. She tried very hard.

Then she lay down on the floor and watched. "Woof," said Katie quietly.

Ruby ran into the kitchen and started to eat Katie's food. That's MY food! thought Katie. She was about to chase Ruby away from her bowl. She tried to hold herself back. She tried very hard.

Then she lay down on the floor and watched Ruby eat. Katie grumbled quietly.

Ruby ran out of the kitchen. Katie heard SQUEAK SQUEAK SQUEAK from the other room. Ruby was playing with Katie's squeaky bone! Katie wanted to take it away from Ruby. She tried to hold herself back. She tried very hard.

Then she lay down on the floor and watched Ruby chew on her toy. Katie sighed.

Ruby walked over to Katie and
dropped the toy in front of her.

Katie picked it up in her mouth. Then Ruby grabbed the other end and pulled. Katie pulled back. Ruby pulled back. Katie pulled back.

Soon Katie and Ruby were having a
tug-of-war. This is fun! thought Katie as
they spun in circles.

Katie dropped the toy and ran
around and around the room.
"AROOOOO!" she howled.

Ruby chased her. "Yip! Yip! Yip!" she barked. They chased each other through every room in the house.

Soon they were thirsty and tired.
LAP LAP LAP went their tongues as the
two dogs drank side by side.

Katie walked over to her pillow and plopped down with the cats. Ruby watched her. Katie moved over to make room for her new friend.